Brave Bear

Kathy Mallat

Walker and Company
New York

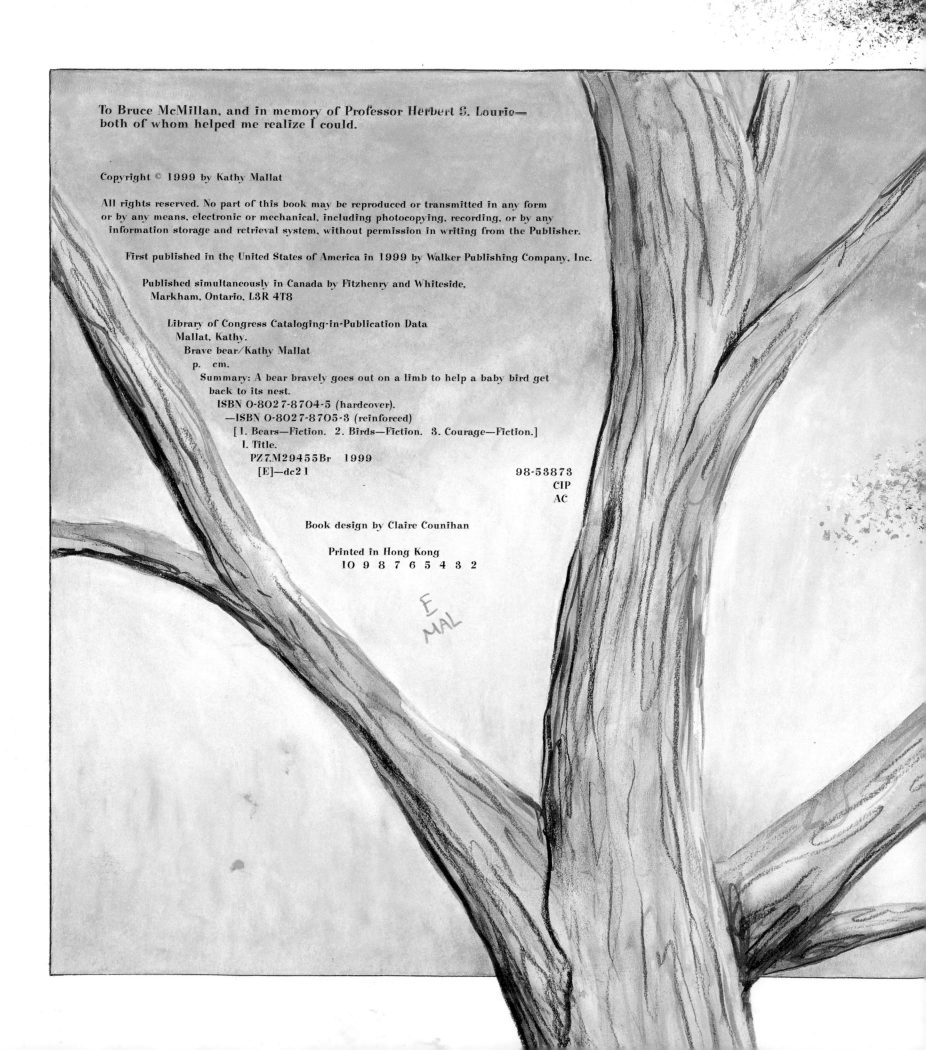

To Bruce McMillan, and in memory of Professor Herbert S. Lourie—
both of whom helped me realize I could.

First published in the United States of America in 1999 by Walker Publishing Company, Inc.

Published simultaneously in Canada by Fitzhenry and Whiteside,
Markham, Ontario, L3R 4T8

Library of Congress Cataloging-in-Publication Data
Mallat, Kathy.
Brave bear/Kathy Mallat
p. cm.
Summary: A bear bravely goes out on a limb to help a baby bird get
back to its nest.
ISBN 0-8027-8704-5 (hardcover).
—ISBN 0-8027-8705-3 (reinforced)
[1. Bears—Fiction. 2. Birds—Fiction. 3. Courage—Fiction.]
I. Title.
PZ7.M29455Br 1999
[E]—dc21   98-53873
                                                       CIP
                                                       AC

Book design by Claire Counihan

Printed in Hong Kong
10 9 8 7 6 5 4 3 2

E
MAL

Are you all right?

Can I help you?

Where?

Over there?

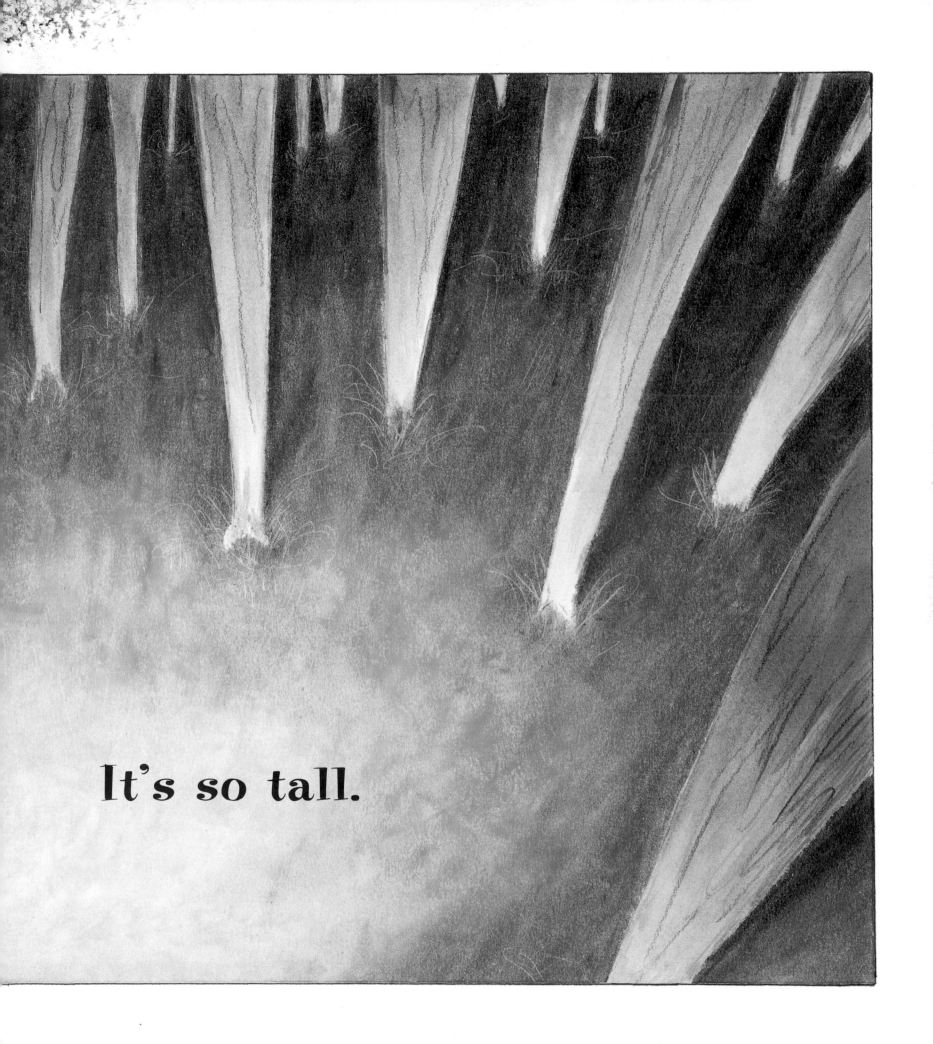

It's so tall.

I'm not sure that I can . . .

but I'll try.

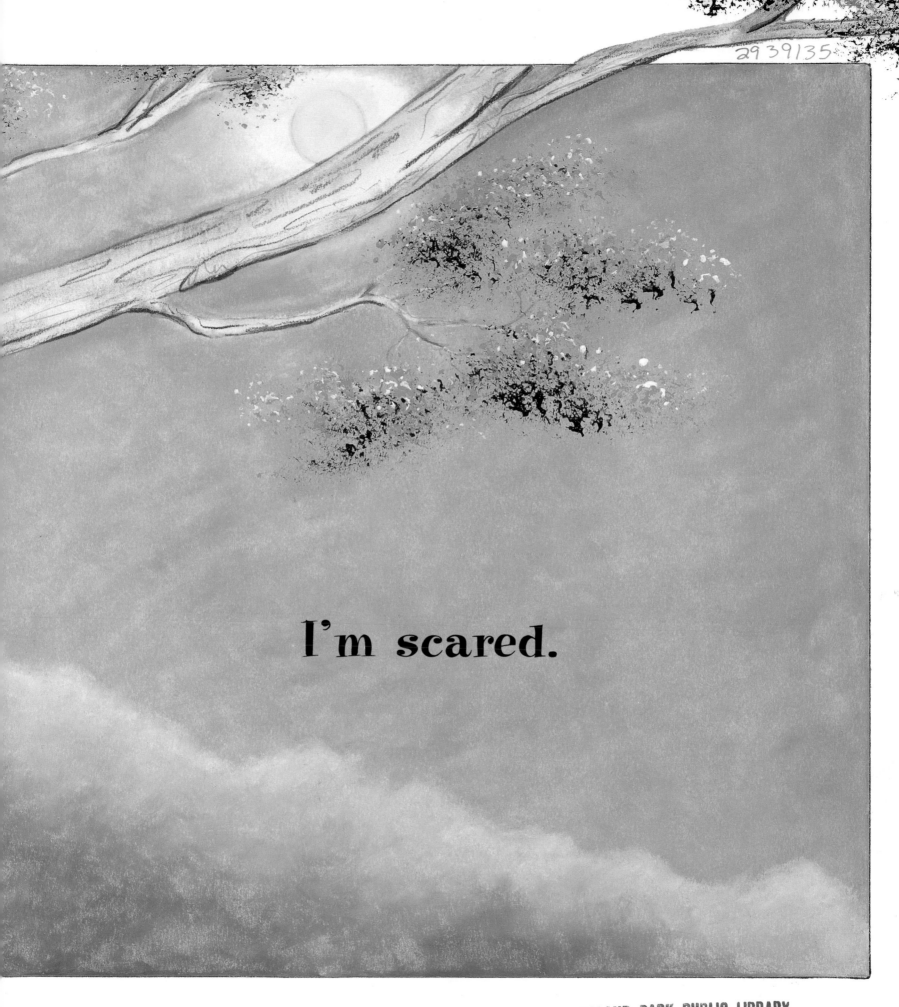

I'm scared.

I need help.

Thanks.

We're almost there.

I'm sure I can.

I did.

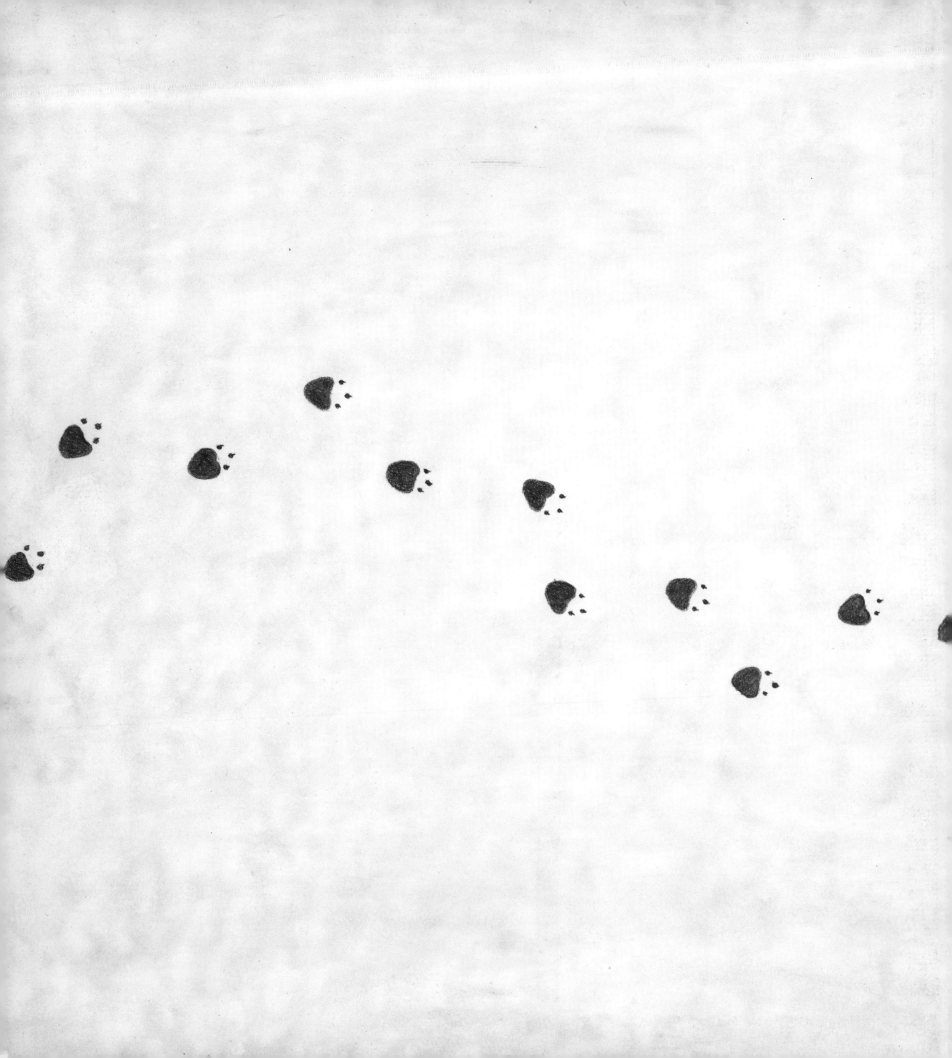